A story about
a small dog
facing a BIG challenge
with a solution
as light as a feather

For Ella and Anya

Special thanks to
Amelia and Penny

Copyright © 2018 by Terry Milne

First U.S. edition 2019
First published by Old Barn Books (United Kingdom) 2018 as Charlie Star

Library of Congress Catalog Card Number pending
ISBN 978-1-5362-0916-7

19 20 21 22 23 24 TWP 10 9 8 7 6 5 4 3 2 1

Printed in Johor Bahru, Malaysia

This book was typeset in Wes Regular.
The illustrations were created in ink and watercolor wash.

Candlewick Press
99 Dover Street
Somerville, Massachusetts 02144

visit us at www.candlewick.com

MIX
Paper from
responsible sources
FSC® C012700

Every morning,
Charlie hopped out of bed.
One, two, three . . . Hop like a flea.

He balanced his toast.
Four, five, six . . . Charlie likes his tricks.

And he watered his plants.
Seven, eight, nine . . . All in a line.

Every day, Charlie
walked once around the
fire hydrant on his way
to the market.

And he always walked on the same side of the old oak tree.

Charlie did everything the same, every day.
He was afraid something bad would happen if he didn't.

At bedtime,
Charlie checked
under the bed . . .

and behind
the curtains.

And he arranged his toys in a neat row:

"All into bed, Rabbit, Panda, Ted,
to keep us lucky, Dog, Doll, and Ducky."

When he would finally lie down,
Charlie always had the same thought:

"I REMEMBERED EVERYTHING TODAY,
AND THINGS TURNED OUT OK!"

Early one morning, the phone rang.

RRRRRiiiNGG, RRRRiiiiNGG!

Charlie leaped out of bed
and ran to pick it up.

He was in such a rush, he forgot to hop.

QUACK, QUACK, QUACK!

It was Duck.

Their friend Hans was stuck.

"I'll be right there," said Charlie.

Four, five, six . . . I must do my tricks.

OOPS!

Seven, eight, nine . . . It's going to be fine.

Duck and Charlie rushed past the fire hydrant
and went the wrong way around the old oak tree.
Charlie wanted to start all over again, but his friend needed him.

"We were playing hide-and-seek,"
said Big Bruce, "but Hans got stuck.
We tried everything we could think of to free him."

They had tried to ROLL
Hans out of the pipe.

They had tried to PUSH
him through the pipe.

They had tried to PULL
him out of the pipe.

"But nothing worked," said Bruce.

"So we called you."

Charlie looked into the dark pipe.

And then he had an idea.

WOOF, WOOF!

TEE-HEE!
HA, HA, HA
HO, HO
TEE-H

Charlie tickled,
and Hans giggled.

Hans wiggled and
wriggled and jiggled
and giggled until . . .

"Thanks, Charlie,"
said Hans. "You're a star!"

"Quack, quack, quack!"
agreed Duck.

Cat said,
"Let's play
Simon Says."

"Yeah!"
replied the others.

And they played
all afternoon.

On his way home, Charlie felt so happy
that he didn't think about which way
he passed the old oak tree.

He flopped into bed with a new thought in his head.

"I FORGOT EVERYTHING TODAY,
BUT THINGS TURNED OUT OK."

The next morning,
Charlie hopped out of bed.
One, two, three . . . Hop like a flea.

He balanced his toast.
Four, five, six . . . Charlie likes his tricks.

And he watered his plants.
Seven, eight, nine . . . All in a line.

On his way to the market,
he went once around the fire hydrant.
Then he skipped any old way past the old oak tree.
Charlie knew that nothing bad would happen,
and maybe what did happen . . .

would be

wonderful!